Dear Family Members,

Just as your child grows inch by inch, your child's reading skills grow word by word. You and your child will enjoy every word in this book because each one has its own special page. This set-up will help your child learn that words and pictures have meaning.

Your child will also come to understand an important concept about how speech and print are different:

Iloveyou—sounds like this.
I love you—looks like this.

Concepts like this one help your child grow as a reader. These skills, when combined with decoding and understanding stories, will lead to reading success.

Remember, the most important part of family reading time is in a word—YOU!

Happy Reading,

Francie Alexander
Chief Education Officer,
Scholastic Education

Three Tips to Get Started:

1. *Before* reading, look at the cover, and talk about what you will read together.
2. *During* reading, read each word and talk about the story.
3. *After* reading, let your child choose a favorite word and make a picture to illustrate it. You and your child can make your own word by word reader!

For all the kids who love milk
and cookies!
—M.R.

Copyright © 2002 by Michael Rex.
All rights reserved. Published by Scholastic Inc.
SCHOLASTIC, WORD BY WORD FIRST READER, CARTWHEEL BOOKS,
and associated logos are trademarks and/or
registered trademarks of Scholastic Inc.

Library of Congress Cataloging-in-Publication Data
Rex, Michael.
    Santa's busy night / by Michael Rex.
        p.   cm. — (Word by word first reader)
    Summary: An elf helps Santa on Christmas Eve.
    ISBN 0-439-33491-8 (pbk)
    [1. Santa Claus— Fiction. 2. Christmas—Fiction. 3. Elves—Fiction] I. Title. II. Series

    PZ7.R32875 San 2002
[E]— dc21   2001049144

10 9 8 7 6 5 4   03 04 05 06
            Printed in the U.S.A.   23
            First printing, October 2002

Santa's Busy Night

by Michael Rex

Cartwheel
·B·O·O·K·S·®

SCHOLASTIC INC.

New York   Toronto   London   Auckland   Sydney
Mexico City   New Delhi   Hong Kong   Buenos Aires

Look!

Coat.

Boots.

Gloves.

Hat.

List.

Bag.

Toys.

Sleigh.

Fly.

Land.

Chimney.

Stuck!

Push.

Down.

Out!

Dirty.

Clean.

No!

Switch.

Tree.

Under.

Bump.

Fall.

Catch!

Fix.

Cookies.

Milk.

Yum!